Dear Parents:

Congratulations! Your child is taking the first steps on an exciting journey. The destination? Independent reading!

STEP INTO READING® will help your child get there. The program offers five steps to reading success. Each step includes fun stories and colorful art or photographs. In addition to original fiction and books with favorite characters, there are Step into Reading Non-Fiction Readers, Phonics Readers and Boxed Sets, Sticker Readers, and Comic Readers—a complete literacy program with something to interest every child.

Learning to Read, Step by Step!

Ready to Read   Preschool–Kindergarten
• big type and easy words • rhyme and rhythm • picture clues
For children who know the alphabet and are eager to begin reading.

Reading with Help   Preschool–Grade 1
• basic vocabulary • short sentences • simple stories
For children who recognize familiar words and sound out new words with help.

Reading on Your Own   Grades 1–3
• engaging characters • easy-to-follow plots • popular topics
For children who are ready to read on their own.

Reading Paragraphs   Grades 2–3
• challenging vocabulary • short paragraphs • exciting stories
For newly independent readers who read simple sentences with confidence.

Ready for Chapters   Grades 2–4
• chapters • longer paragraphs • full-color art
For children who want to take the plunge into chapter books but still like colorful pictures.

STEP INTO READING® is designed to give every child a successful reading experience. The grade levels are only guides; children will progress through the steps at their own speed, developing confidence in their reading.

Remember, a lifetime love of reading starts with a single step!

Visit us on the Web!
StepIntoReading.com
randomhousekids.com

Educators and librarians, for a variety of teaching tools, visit us at RHTeachersLibrarians.com

ISBN 978-0-553-50866-6 (trade) — ISBN 978-0-553-50867-3 (lib. bdg.)

Printed in the United States of America   10 9 8 7 6 5 4 3 2 1

Random House Children's Books supports the First Amendment and celebrates the right to read.

Too Much Ooze!

illustrated by Patrick Spaziante

Random House 🏠 New York

The Kraang are invaders from another world.

They make
a green goo
called mutagen.

Mutagen splashes on
four small turtles.
They grow.

They become
the Teenage Mutant
Ninja Turtles.

Shredder is the Turtles'
most dangerous enemy.

Shredder is

an evil ninja master.

Many bad guys help him.

Shredder has a plan.
He gets mutagen
from the Kraang.

Shredder wants
to mutate everyone
in New York City!

The Turtles must
stop Shredder.

Leo leads
his brothers
into battle!

The bad guys fight
the Turtles.

Mikey kicks.

Raph jumps.

One bad guy
knocks over
the mutagen!

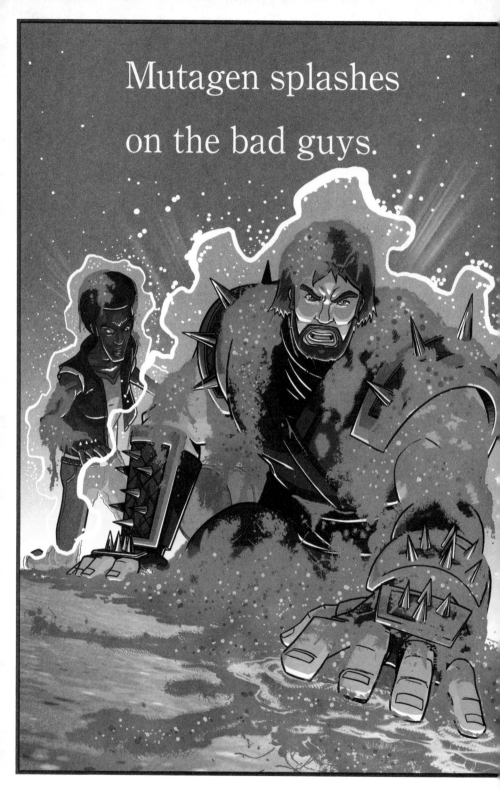

Mutagen splashes
on the bad guys.

They change into

mutants named

Dogpound and Fishface!

The Turtles escape.

Shredder's plan is ruined.

The bad guys
will fight the Turtles
another day.

Turtle Power!